MR. GREEDY

by Roger Hargreaves

Mr Greedy liked to eat!

In fact Mr Greedy loved to eat, and the more he ate the fatter he became.

And the trouble was, the fatter he became the more hungry he became.

And the more hungry he became the more he ate.

And the more he ate the fatter he became.

And so it went on.

Mr Greedy lived in a house that looked rather like himself.

It was a roly-poly sort of a house.

One morning Mr Greedy awoke rather earlier than usual.

He'd been dreaming about food, as usual, and that had made him wake up feeling hungry, as usual.

So Mr Greedy got up, went downstairs and ate the most enormous breakfast.

This is what Mr Greedy had for his breakfast.

TOAST – 2 slices

CORNFLAKES – 1 packet

MILK – 1 bottle

SUGAR – 1 bowlful

TOAST – 3 slices

EGGS – 3 boiled

TOAST – 4 slices

BUTTER – 1 dish

MARMALADE – 1 pot

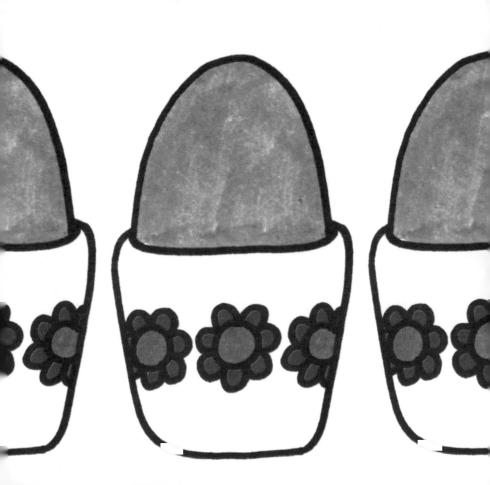

When he had finished his enormous breakfast, Mr Greedy sat back in his chair, smiled a very satisfied smile, and thought.

"That was a delicious breakfast," he thought to himself. "Now I wonder what would be nice to have for lunch?"

He decided in order to work up an appetite for lunch he would go for a long walk.

That morning Mr Greedy walked and walked and walked.

Then he discovered a cave.

"That's funny," he thought, "I don't remember seeing that there before."

Mr Greedy, being a curious sort of a fellow, decided to explore.

He entered the dark cave.

Inside he discovered some giant steps leading upwards.

Mr Greedy, being a curious sort of a fellow, decided to climb them.

They were very steep and very difficult to climb, but with much huffing and puffing Mr Greedy climbed up and up.

At the top of the steps Mr Greedy came to a door.

It was, without doubt, the biggest door that Mr Greedy had ever seen. And it wasn't quite shut.

Mr Greedy, being a curious sort of a fellow, decided to see what was on the other side of that door.

So Mr Greedy squeezed himself through the crack in the door, and there before him was an amazing sight.

The biggest room in the world!

The floor was as big as a field.

The table in the middle of the floor was as big as a house, and the chairs around it were as high as trees.

Mr Greedy felt very small.

Then he sniffed.

Coming from somewhere up on top of that gigantic table was the most delicious foody smell that Mr Greedy had ever smelled.

Mr Greedy sniffed again, and then decided that he must get up on to that table, so he began to climb up the leg of the enormous chair.

It was very difficult and it took him a long time, but eventually Mr Greedy stood on the table.

Everything was larger than life.

The salt and pepper pots were both as big as pillar boxes.

There was a bowl of fruit on the table, and Mr Greedy tried to lift one of the oranges.

And Mr Greedy, being Mr Greedy, took a bite out of one of the apples there.

Then he looked around.

Over on the other side of the table stood the source of that delicious smell.

A huge enormous gigantic colossal plate, and on the plate, huge enormous gigantic colossal sausages the size of pillows, and huge enormous gigantic colossal potatoes the size of beachballs, and huge enormous gigantic colossal peas the size of cabbages.

Mr Greedy hurried across the table towards the plate, and, being Mr Greedy, began to eat.

Suddenly a shadow fell across the plate, and Mr Greedy found himself being picked up by a giant hand and looking into the eyes of a real live giant.

"AND WHO," thundered the giant, "ARE YOU?"

Mr Greedy was so frightened that he could only just manage to squeak his name. "Mr Greedy," he squeaked.

The giant laughed a laugh as loud as thunder. "GREEDY BY NAME AND GREEDY BY NATURE," he bellowed. "WELL I THINK MR GREEDY THAT YOU NEED TO BE TAUGHT A LESSON!"

And what a lesson it was.

The giant made Mr Greedy eat up everything on that huge enormous gigantic colossal plate.

When he had finished, Mr Greedy felt very ill indeed, as if he would burst at any minute.

"Now," said the giant in a much quieter voice, "do you promise never to be greedy again?"

"Oh yes," moaned Mr Greedy, "I promise!"

"Very well," said the giant, "then I'll let you go."

Mr Greedy climbed down from the table and went out through the door feeling very fat and extremely miserable.

And do you know, from that day to this, Mr Greedy has kept his promise.

And do you know something else as well?

Mr Greedy doesn't look like he used to look any more.

He now looks like this, which I think suits him a lot better, don't you?

So if you know anybody who's as greedy as Mr Greedy used to be you know what to tell them, don't you?

Beware of giants!

3 Great Offers for MR.MEN Fans!

MR.MEN TOKEN

1 New Mr. Men or Little Miss Library Bus Presentation Cases

A brand new stronger, roomier school bus library box, with sturdy carrying handle and stay-closed fasteners.
The full colour, wipe-clean boxes make a great home for your full collection.
They're just £5.99 inc P&P and free bookmark!

☐ MR. MEN   ☐ LITTLE MISS (please tick and order overleaf)

2 Door Hangers and Posters

PLEASE STICK YOUR 50P COIN HERE

In every Mr. Men and Little Miss book like this one, you will find a special token. Collect 6 tokens and we will send you a brilliant Mr. Men or Little Miss poster and a Mr. Men or Little Miss double sided full colour bedroom door hanger of your choice. Simply tick your choice in the list and tape a 50p coin for your two items to this page.

Door Hangers (please tick)
☐ Mr. Nosey & Mr. Muddle
☐ Mr. Slow & Mr. Busy
☐ Mr. Messy & Mr. Quiet
☐ Mr. Perfect & Mr. Forgetful
☐ Little Miss Fun & Little Miss Late
☐ Little Miss Helpful & Little Miss Tidy
☐ Little Miss Busy & Little Miss Brainy
☐ Little Miss Star & Little Miss Fun

Posters (please tick)
☐ MR.MEN
☐ LITTLE MISS

3 Sixteen Beautiful Fridge Magnets – any 2 for £2.00!
inc.P&P

They're very special collector's items!
Simply tick your first and second* choices from the list below
of any 2 characters!

1st Choice

- [ ] Mr. Happy
- [ ] Mr. Lazy
- [ ] Mr. Topsy-Turvy
- [ ] Mr. Bounce
- [ ] Mr. Bump
- [ ] Mr. Small
- [ ] Mr. Snow
- [ ] Mr. Wrong

- [ ] Mr. Daydream
- [ ] Mr. Tickle
- [ ] Mr. Greedy
- [ ] Mr. Funny
- [ ] Little Miss Giggles
- [ ] Little Miss Splendid
- [ ] Little Miss Naughty
- [ ] Little Miss Sunshine

2nd Choice

- [ ] Mr. Happy
- [ ] Mr. Lazy
- [ ] Mr. Topsy-Turvy
- [ ] Mr. Bounce
- [ ] Mr. Bump
- [ ] Mr. Small
- [ ] Mr. Snow
- [ ] Mr. Wrong

- [ ] Mr. Daydream
- [ ] Mr. Tickle
- [ ] Mr. Greedy
- [ ] Mr. Funny
- [ ] Little Miss Giggles
- [ ] Little Miss Splendid
- [ ] Little Miss Naughty
- [ ] Little Miss Sunshine

*Only in case your first choice is out of stock.

---- TO BE COMPLETED BY AN ADULT ----

To apply for any of these great offers, ask an adult to complete the coupon below and send it with the appropriate payment and tokens, if needed, to MR. MEN OFFERS, PO BOX 7, MANCHESTER M19 2HD

- [ ] Please send ____ Mr. Men Library case(s) and/or ____ Little Miss Library case(s) at £5.99 each inc P&P
- [ ] Please send a poster and door hanger as selected overleaf. I enclose six tokens plus a 50p coin for P&P
- [ ] Please send me ____ pair(s) of Mr. Men/Little Miss fridge magnets, as selected above at £2.00 inc P&P

Fan's Name _____

Address _____

_____ **Postcode** _____

Date of Birth _____

Name of Parent/Guardian _____

Total amount enclosed £ _____

- [ ] **I enclose a cheque/postal order payable to Egmont Books Limited**
- [ ] **Please charge my MasterCard/Visa/Amex/Switch or Delta account** (delete as appropriate)

Card Number

Expiry date ___/___ **Signature** _____

MR.MEN   LITTLE MISS
Mr. Men and Little Miss™ & ©Mrs. Roger Hargreaves